HARLEQUIN & MOTHER GOOSE

or The Magic Stick

By Ruth Robbins Illustrated by Nicolas Sidjakov
Parnassus Press, Berkeley, California

Copyright 1965 by Ruth Robbins for story, by Nicolas Sidjakov for illustrations.
Library of Congress Catalog Card Number 65-22429.
Published by Parnassus Press. Lithographed in the United States of America.

Once there was a young man, a daring, witty and gay young man named Harlequin. Harlequin would rather dance than walk; he would rather caper like a clown than stroll like an ordinary fellow. Harlequin could run like a deer; he could twirl like a top; he could leap like a flame in the wind. His suit dazzled the eye with color. Silver buckles adorned his soft leather slippers, and he carried a flat wooden sword, a slapstick. If Harlequin wanted to play a trick or pretend a disguise he wore a mask. There was mischief in his eye and goodness in his heart.

On this particular spring day, however, Harlequin sat motionless at the doorstep of a little house in the woods, the house of his friend Mother Goose, waiting for her to return home. As he sat, tears flowed over his cheeks, trickled from the tip of his nose, and ran down to his toes. An owl, guarding the door, stared solemnly at Harlequin.

Presently, a clear, thin voice sang through the treetops:

Old Mother Goose
When she wanted to wander,
Would ride through the air
On a very fine gander.

Harlequin looked up to see Mother Goose riding down from the sky on her gander. She laughed at the sight of Harlequin but was puzzled when she saw his tears.

"Harlequin, my dancing friend, what makes you sad today?"

"Ah, good Mother, such grief I have never known before. I love sweet Columbine. She is fair and beautiful, and she returns my love. But her uncle, Pantaloon, thinks me a poor and foolish fellow, and he will not let us marry. What am I to do?" The tears came fresh now, rolling off the point of his chin. The owl blinked three times.

"You are not poor in deeds and spirit, this I know," said Mother Goose. "And maybe it is foolish to love Sweet Columbine whose uncle will not have you. But we shall see. That miser Pantaloon may soon change his mind."

From her small house she led forth a large white goose. "Take this fine goose, Harlequin. She will lay a Golden Egg each day. Promise to care for her well, to treat her gently, and she is yours. Ha!" the old woman chuckled, "Pantaloon may think better of you when he sees what you possess. Now be off! Go and win your lady."

Harlequin swung Mother Goose round and round until her skirts ballooned about her. Then with one quick step he lighted upon the back of the white goose and flew off to the house of Columbine and Pantaloon.

Columbine sat in her garden, a princess among fair maidens. Her dress was of finest soft linen, and a garland of spring flowers crowned her hair. Her face glowed like a sunlit blossom when she saw Harlequin.

Pantaloon bustled out from behind a hedge. His jowl shook, and his stomach bounced in tight breeches as he hurried toward the two young lovers. Harlequin bowed low to the old man. "Pantaloon, sir, I have here an egg of pure gold just laid by this wonderful goose. The egg is yours if you will give me the hand of fair Columbine."

Pantaloon looked with admiration at the oval of gold Harlequin held out to him. "What a treasure!" he murmured, rubbing his pudgy hands. He looked at the goose, then back at the shining egg. His body quivered with anticipation. "I will have both the egg *and* the goose."

"I can give you the egg only," said Harlequin. "But what a jewel it is, see?" He spun the Golden Egg on the end of one finger.

Pantaloon pulled Columbine toward him. "The egg and the goose, nothing less!"

Poor Harlequin. How could he give up this magic gift entrusted to him? "Sir," he pleaded, "the Golden Egg is all I dare offer."

Pantaloon trembled with anger. "The egg *and* the goose, I say! Then you may marry my niece."

Alas, poor Harlequin. His heart ached now at the sight of Sweet Columbine's tears. "Very well, the goose is yours, for I will have my lady."

No sooner were the white goose and the Golden Egg in the clutches of Pantaloon than the old man laughed aloud. "Now *all* the golden eggs are mine. And why not all at once? Yes, I will be rich today!" He pulled a dagger from his belt and swung it high, about to kill the remarkable bird.

There was a flash of wings and Mother Goose appeared. With one lightning stroke she rescued the goose and snatched the Golden Egg from Pantaloon. "You are too greedy, old man!" she shrieked at him. "And you, Harlequin, could you not see your folly? Love is blind. You have broken your promise, and I take back the white goose. But you must pay for your mistake. I shall throw the Golden Egg into the sea. You and Columbine will flee from here in search of the egg." She lifted her head and cackled. "And a desperate chase it will be, with Pantaloon in pursuit.

Only when you recover the Golden Egg, Harlequin, and bring it to me, will you be at rest and have your Columbine." She turned to go, then paused. "But since you are my friend and kind in heart I will give you one aid in your quest." She touched his stick with a bony forefinger. "Your slapstick is now a magic wand. Guard this gift better than you did the first, and it will serve you well. Now fly!"

And so it happened. As if suddenly caught in the spell of the old woman's words, Harlequin and Columbine fled from the garden; and Pantaloon, enraged by the loss of the gold and his niece, ran after them as fast as his short legs could take him.

With feet barely touching the ground, the young pair raced over hills and downs. They danced over stone stiles and across bubbling freshets. White sails of a windmill creaked a slow circle on the morning breeze, and the landscape became a patchwork of green velvet rolling on forever.

A good distance later they came breathless upon a humble farm house. The farmer's kind wife sat at her spinning wheel in the doorway. Harlequin asked for a place to hide from their pursuer, and the kind wife led them to a barn behind the cottage. She pointed to a haystack. "Poor though it is, you are welcome to rest here." Then she gasped in alarm at the sudden loud rattling of the front gate, followed by stamping and shouting.

Pantaloon's voice boomed into the farmyard. "Harlequin and Columbine I've caught up with you...let me in I say!"

"'Tis a pity," said Kind Wife. That moment Harlequin leaped high into the air and performed three perfect spins. He waved his Magic Stick, and the stick sang out:

Little Boy Blue,
Come blow your horn,
The sheep's in the meadow,
The cow's in the corn.

Where is the boy
Who looks after the sheep?
He's under a haycock
Fast asleep.

Little Boy Blue crawled out from under the haycock and rubbed his eyes. He shook himself free of straw and began to blow his horn. As the first notes sounded, golden coins began to spill out of the horn. Pantaloon came puffing into the barnyard. Poor Farmer came running after him. Boy Blue played on while the coins pouring from his horn formed a small mound, then a larger one. Poor Farmer and his Kind Wife danced a merry jig around the shower of wealth before them. Pantaloon could not move his gaze from the growing heap of gold. Chickens, pigs, goats scurried about the barnyard clucking, grunting and bleating.

In all the hub-bub, Harlequin and Columbine tiptoed quietly out of the yard. Who knows how long it took Pantaloon to pull himself away from the sight of that glittering fortune? Indeed, it was a torture. But when he finally raised his eyes, Harlequin and

LITTLE BOY BLUE
COME BLOW YOUR HORN THE
SHEEP'S IN THE MEADOW
THE COW'S
IN
THE
CORN

Columbine had vanished from his view.

The two raced across cool meadows and under blossoming trees. Their shadows rippled ahead of them on the pebbled road. Presently they saw a chairmender trudging toward them, his body bent under a tower of chairs and odd pieces strapped to his back.

Said Harlequin, "My good fellow, pray tell us if we are traveling the shortest way to the sea." And the chairmender answered, "Follow this road beyond the village, then through the woods, then a good half league beyond that, and there you will meet the sea."

Harlequin, graceful as a cat, climbed to the topmost chair on the tradesman's back, balanced himself for a moment, then leaped to the road in a sweeping bow. Columbine, too, thanked the chairmender with a low curtsy, and the two continued on their way.

The road grew wider and easier; they hastened past houses with trim gardens shining in the sunlight. Soon they were entering a small village.

Harlequin and Columbine hurried through the empty village streets. Hand in hand they danced along rooftops toward the strains of music and the hum of people gathered together; the sounds of a country fair beckoned them until, at last, they came upon the crowded village square. Children, mothers, fathers, grandfathers, uncles and aunts were there. Milkmaids, tinkers, candlers, bakers, fishmongers, and knifegrinders were there. Streamers fluttered over the stalls where tradespeople shouted their wares. Wheels of chance twirled in the air like giant pinwheels.

Said Harlequin to Columbine, "This country fair will help us hide for a while." He pushed through a jumble of people toward one corner of the square. There, a small stage was built on stilts with a curtain spread behind, and on the platform a group of musicians played for the entertainment of the fairgoers.

Above the sound of fiddle, pipe and lute, the din of voices, the bustle of petticoats, Columbine heard a distant yet familiar cry. "It's Pantaloon! Oh Harlequin, my uncle still follows us."

"Even in this throng he smells us out." Harlequin looked back over the heads of the people. "Quick, dear Columbine, up on the platform." He leaped with Columbine in his arms. "Wait here, behind the curtain, while I take the stage. I will give Pantaloon and the townspeople a good show. And perhaps we can escape your uncle, yet."

Harlequin fixed his half-mask to his face and bounced on to the stage. In less than an instant he leaped in three high arcs, spun his body into a dazzling rainbow of color and ended with a deep bow. The crowd answered with cheering and clapping.

Now Harlequin turned to a small table behind him, and on the table he saw a bowl of steaming soup. With a flip of his hand, his pantomime act began. He picked up the bowl and drank the soup, then fanned his tongue. When he returned the bowl to the table he found a plate of spaghetti in its place, took up the spaghetti and quickly began to eat it. The long white strings of paste stuck to his hands and face. When he had untangled himself from the last sticky strand, he turned to the table with the empty plate only to find the bowl filled with piping hot soup. He immediately gulped all the soup with one swallow, but not fast enough, for spaghetti already overflowed the plate. Faster and faster Harlequin devoured the food; faster and faster the bowl and the plate refilled with soup and spaghetti. Harlequin twisted, he fell, he tumbled, he rolled, he grinned, he scowled, until the audience cried with delight at this gay buffoon of a fellow.

Pantaloon, in the audience, recognized Harlequin at last. His face flushed purple. He squeezed his round body forward toward the stage, shaking a fist and sputtering, "Hold him! hold him!" Harlequin, alarmed at the energy of this stout gentleman, swung far back and quickly waved his Magic Stick. The crowd quieted as the stick sang out:

> *Tom, he was a piper's son,*
> *He learned to play when he was young,*
> *But all the tunes that he could play*
> *Was, 'Over the hills and far away'.*

On the stage the piper played to the tune of the Magic Stick:

> *Tom, with his pipe made such a noise,*
> *That he pleased both the girls and boys;*
> *They all danced while he did play,*
> *'Over the hills and far away'.*

The children laughed and shouted and jumped. They clambered over Pantaloon and crowded round the piper, pulling him down from the stage. Pantaloon could not move; he was caught in the jostle of dancing children surrounding the piper.

> *Tom with his pipe did play with such skill*
> *That those who heard him could never keep still;*
> *As soon as he played they began for to dance,*
> *Even pigs on their hind legs would after him prance.*

Now the mothers and fathers, grandfathers and uncles and aunts, the milkmaid, the tinker, the candler, the baker, the fishmonger, and the knifegrinder began to dance to the piper's magic tune. Pantaloon was helplessly drawn by the spell of the music. He could not resist dancing; he could only follow the piper who slowly led the merry dancing villagers out of the square, over the hills, and far away.

Harlequin lost not a moment to reach Sweet Columbine who waited, fretting, behind the curtain. He whisked her along with him out of the village, and soon the two lovers were laughing over their escape from Pantaloon. Harlequin somersaulted down the

TOM WITH HIS PIPE MADE SUCH A NOISE THAT HE PLEASED BOTH THE GIRLS AND BOYS THEY ALL DANCED WHILE HE DID PLAY OVER THE HILLS AND FAR AWAY

lane while Columbine tripped gaily beside him.

Their shadows followed them, faster and faster, as the sun dipped toward the horizon. Velvet hills folded and curved ahead, and wild flowers closed their petals against the coming twilight.

A pieman, with his little dog, came whistling along the road. The man carried a large flat tray filled with all sizes of pies, delicate fruit turnovers, and mouth-watering berry tarts. Columbine smelled the good pastry aroma and slowed to a stop, all at once overcome with hunger. She fixed her eyes on the tempting display.

"Come, there is no time my lady," coaxed Harlequin. "We must fly while we can."

"But I am truly famished, dear Harlequin. Just one?"

The pieman, with an inviting smile, urged Columbine to choose what she fancied, and that gentle lady hastily satisfied her appetite with five fruit turnovers, topped by a juicy raspberry tart. Harlequin could not refrain from eating one small golden-crusted pie.

"Ah, delicious food my good man." He paid the vendor three pennies. "Now pray tell us if we travel the shortest route to the sea." And the pieman answered, "Yonder over the hill you will come to the woods. Follow the road through the woods, take no side paths mind you, then continue a good half league beyond that, and there you will come upon the sea."

Harlequin balanced the little dog on his head and blithely

danced a circle around the pie vendor who watched, turning in amazement. The little dog wiggled to the ground, and with a hasty bow and curtsy Harlequin and Columbine hurried on their way.

Far ahead in the fading light they saw their road enter the woods. At the edge of the woods they found an old stone well and stopped for a drink of cool water. "I cannot step another step," said gentle Columbine. "Nor can I leap another leap," answered Harlequin. There, resting against the old stone well, they fell asleep. In the sky a moon of fine silver rose into the night.

A rooster crowed at dawn, and Columbine awakened with a shiver. She heard a muffled sound on the road. When she saw a ball of dust and then a figure in the distance wobbling toward them, she cried out in fright. "Harlequin, wake up! Pantaloon is coming!"

Pantaloon, seeing his niece, began to run. "Columbine, I've caught you now!" he shouted. "And as for you, Mister Harlequin, you will never have your lady." The clap of his boots grew louder. Harlequin sprang to the small roof above the well. With a great flourish of his Magic Stick, the stick sang out:

> *Ride a cock-horse to Banbury Cross,*
> *To see a fine lady upon a white horse;*
> *Rings on her fingers and bells on her toes,*
> *And she shall have music wherever she goes.*

Instantly the thunder of a horse's hooves overtook Pantaloon,

and the Fine Lady, her skirts billowing, her bells jingling, rode toward Harlequin on her beautiful white horse.

"May we ride with you Fine Lady?" implored Harlequin. "We are beset by danger. A greedy, tireless old goat chases us to tear apart our love, and we are lost without your help."

"Climb up quickly . . . make haste," replied the lady of the rings and bells. She held out a hand to Columbine, who scrambled up on the back of the white horse just as Pantaloon reached out to grab his niece. "Ho ho," laughed Harlequin. In a twinkling he jumped from the roof and pushed the miser backward. Pantaloon's pompous figure stuck snugly in the well, and there, half sitting--half leaning, arms and legs fanning the air, he stayed.

Harlequin climbed up behind the Fine Lady. With a ring and a jingle and a jangle, the three rode into the green woods on the back of the white steed. Through the woods and over the rolling hills they raced, down to the edge of the sea. The beautiful white horse stopped short at the rocky coast. Harlequin and Columbine alighted, and before they could thank the Fine Lady she was riding away at a gallop, rings and bells singing on the air.

Sea foam lipped over the sand; waves, pounding against the rocks, spewed fountains of water into the air. On the water's edge the two travelers found a cave for shelter. Columbine began to weep. "The Golden Egg, oh how can we ever find the Golden Egg in this endless sea?" Harlequin tried to comfort his Columbine but

he sensed that time was short before Pantaloon would find them. He looked across the water and, with a hopeless shrug of his shoulders, waved, once more, his Magic Stick.

As the stick flashed an arc through the air, Harlequin heard a strange, gurgling sound. A great fish, larger than anyone had ever seen, bubbled up out of the sea and said, "Know me by the name of Odd Fish. I have been waiting, Harlequin and Columbine. And you have found my cave at last. Welcome."

Harlequin raised his arms toward Odd Fish. "We have run, raced, galloped for our very lives. Our bones ache and our hearts grow weary. Now that we are here, great fish, how are we to find that charm we seek, to end this desperate chase?"

Odd Fish rolled and heaved. His belly glistened with a silvery light. Three mermaids, shining and dainty, raised their heads out of the water around Odd Fish. "Be not without hope," rumbled the sea monster. "If what you seek is in the sea, we will search for it without delay."

"Will you bring me the Golden Egg?" cried Harlequin. In answer, Odd Fish and his mermaids disappeared into the deep waters. Columbine strained on tiptoe, her eyes peering across the horizon. Sea shells circled her tiny slippers. Harlequin, his body taut, waited … listened. What was that thudding? … not the waves lapping, not the wind. He heard a noise of something scraping and sliding over the rocks. He sprinted toward Columbine and

quickly pulled her back into the cave.

"What? Not Pantaloon, I pray?" The maiden trembled.

"He does not give up, that Pantaloon. I fear he will be here soon." The two heard footsteps crunching through the sand, closer and closer.

"Oh my Harlequin, I feel this will be farewell for us now," wept Columbine. As she spoke, mountains of spray rose into the sky, higher than any eye could follow, and Odd Fish swam up from the bottom of the sea. With one flip of his enormous tail he tossed the Golden Egg into the air, and Harlequin bounded to the edge of the shore to catch the prize. At the same time, the dainty mermaids carried a shimmering veil of seaweed to Columbine and placed it over her head and shoulders.

"Mother Goose," Harlequin cried out. "Wherever you are, hurry! Here is your Golden Egg!"

With a brush of wings and a crackle of laughter, Mother Goose rode down from the sky on her white gander. "Indeed you have found the Golden Egg, dear Harlequin." Her eyes twinkled, her skirt danced, and her hat bobbed up and down. She took the Golden Egg just as Pantaloon, gasping, lumbered up to them with arms outstretched to seize Columbine.

"The spell is broken," chanted Mother Goose. "The chase is over. No need to run, Harlequin and Columbine; Pantaloon pursues you no longer. Stop, I say!"

Pantaloon halted in his tracks. He slumped down on the sand, a heap of sobs and groans. Immediately Harlequin turned three handsprings, while beautiful Columbine fluttered with joy by his side.

"True love shall be rewarded," said Mother Goose. "Come, my favorite sprites, this is a wedding day." The shining, dainty mermaids gathered round the two lovers. Odd Fish swished out of the waves to join them. Mother Goose, holding out a hand toward Pantaloon, continued: "For one so greedy, this Golden Egg is too handsome a reward. But take it now as consolation and to restore good disposition among the three of you."

Pantaloon, confounded then delighted, accepted the Golden Egg. His jowl quivered with pleasure.

The shining, dainty mermaids sang; Odd Fish and Pantaloon danced; and Mother Goose swung gaily on her gander. Harlequin and Columbine joined hands, and they were wed beside the sea. Sweet Columbine's bridal veil of seaweed sparkled like a million diamonds, and Harlequin's heart was happy forever after.

AUTHOR'S NOTE

Harlequin was a famous stage personality of extraordinary talent who lived in the theatres of Europe for over 400 years. He began as a crude, clownish street entertainer in the 15th Century in Bergamo, Italy, although some put his beginnings as early as the ancient Greek theatre, and continued to the 19th Century in England. The role of Harlequin flowered to the pinnacle of theatre art in the Commedia dell'arte, Italian improvised comedy, the popular theatre of the time.

Cavorting across the stages of Italy, France, and later England, Harlequin amused and delighted thousands upon thousands of theatregoers. A Harlequinade usually included several stock characters or masks; Harlequin, Columbine, Pantaloon, Clown, Pierrot. The players traveled from village to hamlet to country fair. Their repertoire was varied and ingeniously impromptu, a treat for the common people as well as the aristocracy.

Over the years the foremost actors of Europe played the role of Harlequin which changed and developed from Arrlechino the yokel, in Italy; to Arlequin the capricious lover, in France; to Harlequin the hero with magic powers, in England. He was neither clown nor jester nor fool. He was himself, Harlequin; merry, sad, sly, droll; wearing mask, slapstick, and diamond-patterned suit; moving his audiences to laughter and tears.

Harlequin enlivened the art of the pantomime, the imitation of all things by gesture alone, often accompanied by written signs and choral singing. Pantomime offered opportunity for great wit and satire, extravagant capers and acrobatics; the Harlequinade became the celebrated entertainment of the day.

So much we see performed has borrowed from Harlequin's many-faceted art; the clown, the acrobat, the mime; the comedy, the drama, and especially the ballet. The institution of Harlequin has given us a rich heritage and a source of inspiration.

This story was inspired by a scenario entitled "Harlequin Mother Goose," a Christmas Pantomime by Thomas Dibdin, performed at Covent Garden, England, December 1806. It ran for 99 nights and history has recorded it as one of the most brilliant and triumphant of Harlequinades.